FLY HIGH, FLY LOW

FLY HIGH FLY LOW

BY
DON FREEMAN

THE VIKING PRESS

This story is for
YOU
and for Ronnie and Laurie
Charlene and Bruce
Marc and Archy
Joan and Mary Jo,
with a nudge to Mudge and Judy

In the beautiful city of San Francisco, a city famous
for its fogs and flowers, cable cars and towers, there
once stood an electric-light sign on top of a tall building, and inside the letter B of this sign there lived
a pigeon.

Before choosing to make his home here this proud
gray pigeon had tried living in many other letters
in the alphabet. Just why he liked the lower loop of
the letter B, no one yet knew.

During the day the wide side walls kept the wind away, and at night the bright lights kept him warm and cozy.

The pigeons who roosted along the ledges of the building across the street thought he was a pretty persnickety pigeon to live where he did. "He's too choosy! He's too choosy!" they would coo.

The only one who never made fun of him was a white-feathered dove. She felt sure he must have a good reason for wanting to live in that letter.

Every morning as soon as the sun came up, these two met in mid-air and together they swerved and swooped down into Union Square Park, where they pecked up their breakfast. Mr. Hi Lee was certain to be there, throwing out crumbs from his large paper sack. He would always greet them by saying, "Good morning, Sid and Midge. How are my two early birds?"

All the birds in the city regarded Mr. Hi Lee as their best friend, and he had nicknames for many of them. Sometimes he brought them hard breadcrumbs and sometimes, as an extra-special treat, day-old cake crumbs from a nearby bakery.

After every crumb was pecked up, the pigeons always circled around Mr. Hi Lee's head, flapping their wings as they flew—which was their way of saying, "Thank you!"

By noontime Sid and Midge could be seen sailing high
in the sky, flying into one cloud and out the other.
Side by side they glided over the bay,

until they could look down and see the Golden Gate
Bridge.

Sid would swoop and fly through the open arches just
to show Midge what a good looper he was.

Then, as the setting sun began painting the sky with a rosy glow, two tuckered-out birds would be slowly winging their way back to the park just in time for supper.

One evening after an especially gay lark in the sky, Sid invited Midge to stay and share his letter B with him.

Across the way pigeons were soon bobbing their heads up and down and cooing, "Whoever heard of birds building a nest in a sign? It'll never do! It'll never do!"

But Sid and Midge went right on building their nest as best they could. They used patches of cloth and strands of string and bits of straw, and gradually there grew a strong nest with a perfect view.

Then one misty morning a few weeks later, just as everything was going along smoothly, something happened which was very upsetting! It occurred right after Sid had flown down to the park to peck up his breakfast. As usual he had left Midge taking her turn sitting on the nest, where there were now two eggs to be kept warm!

Suddenly, like a bolt out of the blue, Midge felt their perch give a terrible lurch! The buildings across the way seemed to sway back and forth. "It's an earth quake!" screeched Midge.

J34034

But no—it was even worse than an earthquake! Their sign was being taken down! One by one the letters were being lowered into a waiting truck below. Midge followed, flapping her wings wildly at the movers, trying to let them know they must not take away her nest! But the men paid no attention to her, until the tallest man stopped and shouted,

"Hold everything! Look here what I've found! Two eggs in a nest! No wonder that pigeon has been making such a fuss!"

"Well, what do you know!" exclaimed another man as he took a peek inside. "We'll sure have to take good care of this letter. Come to think of it, I know of a bakery shop that could use a big letter 'B.' Anyway, we won't be throwing this one away. Come on, men, let's get going!"

Down the hill they went, and far out of sight, with
Midge clinging on with all her might!

You can imagine how Sid felt when he landed back on the cold and empty scaffold later that morning! He stood there dazed and bewildered, wondering where his sign had gone. Where was his Midge? And where, oh where, was their nest with those two precious eggs?

He looked around on all sides, but not a trace of his sign did he see. Suddenly off he flew.

First to the waterfront. Possibly the sign was being loaded onto a boat. Sid was sure that wherever that particular letter 'B' was, there, too, Midge would be. He looked high and he looked low, but not a sign of his letter did he spy.

Next he flew to the uppermost post of the Golden Gate Bridge. He thought perhaps Midge might have passed by that way. But no, not a feather did he find.

While he stood wondering where to search next, an enormous fog bank came rolling in from off the ocean. Like a rampaging flock of sheep, the fog came surging straight toward him!

When Sid saw this he puffed out his chest and
stretched his wings wide and cried, "Who's afraid of
a little breeze? I'll flap my wings and blow the wind
away!"

But the fog rolled silently on, and before Sid knew what had happened he was completely surrounded by a dense, damp grayness. And the faster he flew, the thicker the fog grew, until he could barely see beyond his beak. Down, down he dived, hoping to land on solid ground.

All at once he found himself standing on top of a traf-
fic-light signal right in the busiest part of town!

Once inside the green "Go" signal, Sid began fluffing up his wings, trying to dry them off before going on with his search for Midge.

What Sid didn't know was that his fluffed-up wings hid the word "Go," and no one in the street dared to budge. Soon there was a roar of automobile horns! "People certainly get awfully upset over a little fog!" said Sid as he stuck out his head.

Just then along came a policeman, and when he
blew his whistle—BEEEP! BEEEP!—Sid flew out
like a streak of lightning! At last the traffic could
move on!

By now the fog had changed into rain and everybody
started hopping aboard the cable cars—which is what
people do in San Francisco wherever the hills are too
steep or the weather is too wet.

And that's exactly what Sid did! Under the big bell
on top of the cable car he found a perfect umbrella.

If only the conductor hadn't shouted "Hold on tight! Sharp corner ahead!" and then clanged the bell! The clapper of the bell hit Sid so hard that he fell overboard.

In the street gutter below, all bruised and weary, he hobbled along, muttering to himself, "People! It's all people's fault!"

But then he began to think of the kind man in the park.

Would Mr. Hi Lee be there on such a terrible day as this? Sid tried to spread his wings and fly, but he was too weak. He would have to walk all the way to Union Square.

Fortunately the park was only a couple of blocks
away, and just as Sid hopped up onto the curb he
felt a gentle hand reach down and pick him up.

The next thing Sid knew he was inside Mr. Hi Lee's warm overcoat pocket, where, much to his surprise, he found several sunflower seeds. Right away he began to feel better. He could hardly wait to get on with his search for Midge.

When he peeped out, he saw that the rain had
stopped and warm rays from the sun were beginning
to shine down. Mr. Hi Lee talked to his friend inside
his pocket as he walked along. "Around the corner
from here I know of a bakery where we can get something more for you to eat," he said.

As they neared the shop Mr. Hi Lee noticed some men putting a large letter in the sign above the doorway. "Well, look at that—a new letter B!"

Out popped Sid's head, farther. What was that he heard? It sounded exactly like a certain bird he knew cooing. Could it be?

Yes indeed! It was his very own Midge! She had
stayed with their nest through thick and thin.

Up flew Sid like an arrow shot from a bow. And oh, what a meeting! Such billing and cooing as you've never heard! And no wonder, for their two eggs were just about to hatch!

Out came two tiny beaks breaking through their shells!

And out of the bakery shop came the baker and his customers. They all wanted to know what the excitement was about.

Sid knew that his first duty was to find some food for Midge, so down he flew, and there was Mr. Hi Lee already holding out his hand full of cake crumbs!

After taking the crumbs to Midge, Sid hurried right
back down, and this time he circled around and
around Mr. Hi Lee's head flapping his wings happily.
And we know what he meant by that!

Some time later, when their old neighbors came flying by, they saw Sid and Midge peacefully perched in the lower loop of the letter B and the two little ones in the upper loop. "Oh those lucky birds!" they cooed as they flew away. "Sid certainly did know what he was doing when he chose that letter B!"